Adventures of Petey and Steven

Book Two in the Steven Easy Reader Series

Rita Graham

This work is fictionalized memoir, set in the lovely village of Santa Paula, California. To purchase an autographed copy of this book or to receive information concerning additional books in the series contact the author at

ritagrahamauthor@gmail.com

Dedication

Adventures of Petey and Steven, book two, is dedicated to Chris Binsley, the fictionalized "Chris Benton," in this book and in book one, *Petey and Steven*. Midway through this project, I was struggling to finish. Chris joined us for Thanksgiving dinner that year. We reminisced about the great life of children in lovely Santa Paula, California. Chris said he was looking forward to reading my next book. I knew I had to finish. Even though the major characters of the books are Steven and Chris's brother, T.J., it was Chris Binsley's encouragement on Thanksgiving evening that sparked me to finish. Thanks, Chris.

Acknowledgements

Thank you to the children of Santa Paula who appear in this series: Steven, T.J., Chris, Matt, Cecilia. They are joined now, in book two, by Vince, Aaron, Alan, Bobbie and other great kids. Thanks for the memories, you guys. All of you are grown up now. Some are married. You'll have children of your own soon, so raise them well, as you were brought up so well by your parents.

This book was more difficult to write because the fifth grade year included the events of September 11, 2001. Life changed in the adult world. Parents struggled to maintain normalcy for their children. Thank goodness for grandparents, school, Scouts, Little League, all of which kept fun, beauty and laughter in our lives.

In this sequel, the events were harder to piece together and place in their time frames. I can hear you saying, "That event happened the following year!" Or, "The real story was different!" Okay, you are right! Just keep in mind, it's a fictionalized memoir.

Thank you, Chris Graham, for handling the home computer issues again.

Thank you, Arizona author R.L. Clayton, the first person to encourage me to write a book. Thanks also to my editor, Alexis Powers, a fine lady who motivates writers and helps them complete their work.

Thank you, Matt Kohr, who appears in both books as the fictionalized "Matt Klein." Recently, Matt texted his friend Steven, saying, "I loved your Mom's book; I hope she writes another one." Here it is, Matt! Thank you for the motivation.

And thank you to Steve Gordon Linebaugh of Texas who illustrated and formatted this book. Find Steve at www.artbygordon.com.

Chapter 1

Fifth Grade

School started on a hot August morning. Steven and T.J. had already decided to skateboard down Laurel Road early and when they arrived at school, they'd strap their boards onto their backpacks. T.J.'s brother, Chris, had set them up with some tiny bungee cords that would make it easy.

"That brown lunch sack has a cheese sandwich, some apple slices and a cookie," said Mom, pointing to the little bag on the dining room table, being guarded by their dog Petey.

"Mom, I am not taking lunch. I'm going to buy lunch in the cafeteria," replied the brand new fifth-grader as he went over to hug Petey.

"I love you, Petey," said Steven. "Where's your doll baby?" Petey stormed from the kitchen into the living room where he spotted a yellow tennis ball. He snatched it, whirled around, and ran back to Steven prancing and jumping.

Steven and Petey began a pulling contest with the ball until Petey got it and ran away.

"That's fine. Take the cheese sandwich anyway. It can be a snack."

"No, thank you, Mother," said Steven as he picked up his skateboard and spun the wheel with his finger. "Petey will eat it."

At the sound of his name, Petey ran back to Steven with the ball in his mouth and danced in a circle hoping for more fun. Then the dog saw his blue doll baby in the corner. Petey dropped the tennis ball and grabbed the doll. It was shredded from a pulling contest with Dad yesterday.

Steven grabbed a leg of the wet toy and said, "I've got your doll baby, I've got it!"

Petey tugged hard at his end, his tail wagging furiously.

"Are you sure you guys can have skateboards at school?" Mom asked for the eighth time this morning.

"I am certain," replied Steven, huffing and puffing. "By the end of last year, everybody was bringing them to school, so Mr. Pickerell reversed the ban. We just can't ride them on the school grounds." Steven let go of the toy and Petey stood with the blue doll handing from his mouth, stuffing everywhere on the floor.

Reversed the ban, thought Mom. Wow, Steven's vocabulary is getting very sophisticated.

"Everybody has been talking about it," said Steven. "Skateboards are not against the rules this year."

Okay, thought Mom. After five years of school, including kindergarten, she was tired of guessing what the rules might be on the first day of school. But nice old principal, Mr. Pickerell was gone, replaced by grumpy Mr. Anderson. Well, if Steven and T.J. were wrong about the skateboard rules, she could count on them to do what the principal asked. They were good boys.

Suddenly, the loud scream of a howler monkey pierced the quiet of the morning. Petey let out a bark. Through the glass windows, Steven could see that it was T.J., in the street, ready to roll. T.J.'s old retrievers Kelsey and Maggie were at the Bentons' gate wagging their tails furiously. And Mrs. Benton's new dog, Foxy, bounced like a jack-in-the-box on the sofa behind their picture window, crazed by T.J.'s outburst.

Steven opened his door and let out his own loud response, the screech of some tropical bird. Steven and T.J. had secret jungle animal calls that they used to rouse each other from their houses. The neighbors were used to it, but it still drove the dogs mad.

"Have fun, honey, be good, and talk respectful to everybody. I'll see you at three o-clock, okay?"

"Love you, Mom," yelled Steven on his way out the door, backpack on, dragging the skateboard in his left hand.

The boys jail-braked down the broken asphalt driveway towards the highway and its smooth concrete sidewalk, where they could jump on their boards. Then around Say Road to Laurel Drive and smooth riding all the way to the school yard.

Half-way down, each boy noticed how quiet things seemed. Their buddy Travis wasn't at the corner of Laurel Drive waiting for them. He and T.J.'s brother, Chris, were gone to middle school, had been for a couple of years. So was Kristen Sharp. And Kristen's sister Ally was in high school this year. High school!

Finally, they saw Travis's sister Cecilia up ahead walking with Rebecca Sharp. They were cute little girls, starting third grade.

Without making a plan, both boys sped up. Steven crouched down low on his board and jumped off just as he was passing the girls, sending his board flying ahead in the street. T.J. came up fast on the other side and pinched Cee Cee in the arm as he roared ahead and crashed into Steven's board.

The girls screamed with delight.

"You guys are crazy!" yelled Cecilia.

"Hi, Steven. Hi, T.J. You guys are so cool!" yelled Rebecca.

"You know they have skateboards for girls," said T.J. "You girls should get one and ride to school."

"I have one," Cee Cee told them.

"I have one, too," said Rebecca.

Puzzled at why the girls weren't riding their skateboards to school on opening day, the boys got back on their boards, waved at the girls, and sped on.

Another two blocks went by with no kids that they knew. The boys dodged a couple of cars with mothers driving their kids to school. They did not know those kids. They looked so little. Tiny first-graders, they thought.

At the corner of Hawthorne Street, Matt Klein and his brother Stephen roared up on their boards. Stephen was only in third grade but he was a big as his fifth-grade brother.

They will own football in this town someday, Steven thought.

Michael Forrester and the Payan brothers joined them and suddenly, it was a gang of seven charging onto the school grounds. Oddly, this was the first moment since Steven had left his house that he felt normal.

What was this feeling, about being a fifth-grader, the highest grade in elementary school? Why did he feel uneasy instead of glorious? Was it a sense of duty about being one of the big kids now? Was Steven supposed to be a role model? What would that involve? Would the teachers expect the fifth-graders to be more grown-up? What did it mean? These were among a rush of thoughts and feelings he had.

What Steven did not know, was that T.J., and all his fifth-grade buddies were thinking the exact same thing.

Chapter 2

Three O 'Clock

Dad relaxed on the front patio in a plastic chair, rubbing Petey and rolling a tennis ball to him across the grass. Petey skipped and pranced as he brought the balls back to Dad. Then Dad went to his wood pile for some big sticks and heaved them far into the ivy. Petey attacked like a lion, got the wood and paraded it back to Dad like a prize. Suddenly, Petey took off fast around the side of the yard. He had heard something.

Steven and T.J. came over the low rock wall beside Steven's house, the only place the kids could take a short-cut from school and avoid the winding streets. They had their skateboards strapped to their backpacks, freeing their hands to climb over the wide crumbling wall.

The boys had to cut through two neighbors' yards to come home this way. Nobody cared when they were little second or third-graders. Now, both boys sensed they were too big to be trespassing in people's yards. They might scare somebody's mom or grandmother if they kept it up. Right now, they did not dwell on that. The first day of school in their last year of elementary school had just ended. They wanted to get home and tell their moms all about it.

Petey jumped on the wall and knocked T.J. off into the grass. The dog startled Steven and he tumbled forward. Petey left T.J. and jumped on Steven.

"There's my good dog. I love you Petey!" said Steven.

T.J. sprung over the wall and tackled Petey, turning him over onto the grass and nuzzling his head.

"Petey, I'm glad you're a boy," said T.J. "I can beat you up!"

After some play fighting, Petey ran off to the patio and then both boys saw Dad.

"Hey, Dad!" yelled Steven.

T.J. yelled "Hi, Chris." He had begun calling other kids' dads by their first names. It sounded natural coming from T.J., but Steven felt uncomfortable when he tried it.

"How was the first day at the top of the food chain? I decided to come home early to hear about it. Anybody get paddled on the first day of school?" joked Dad as he resumed throwing sticks for Petey to fetch.

T.J. laughed and said, "You're so old. They don't beat kids at school anymore. I wish they would. Now, they just torture us with time-outs and missed recesses. It's far worse these days. But so far, we each have a clean record."

"What is the world coming to?" laughed Dad. "Hey, Steven, I called your mom and told her I would be home early, so she is staying late at work. You boys want to come inside for some cake? Mom made cake last night."

Steven joked "T.J. can only have cake with a plastic fork. Mom said every time she gives him cake, the fork disappears. Matter of fact, I found two of them in the ivy last week."

T.J. looked at Mr. Graham to see if he was in trouble. He wasn't, and Petey nuzzled T.J. in a show of support. T.J. threw his arms around the Grahams' dog.

T.J. said, "Do you know, when I stashed all those forks, I discovered hundreds of Petey's yellow tennis balls in the ivy. Someday, thousands of years from now when the archaeologists excavate this area, they will think we all lived in a tennis camp - that served cake."

Dad smiled at that. Steven threw his head back and laughed. "My mother will think that is the funniest thing she ever heard! All we need is a volcanic eruption and it's Pompeii in Santa Paula."

Just as they were about to head into the house, Mr. Benton's silver truck rumbled up from the highway and pulled in at T.J.'s house.

T.J. lit up with a huge smile and waved at his dad.

"Save me some cake. I'll catch you later," he yelled to the Grahams, racing to his dad's truck and hugging him as he got out.

Steven said, "Hey, Mr. Benton came home early today, too. I don't think I've ever seen him home this early."

"Well, this is the first day of your last year at elementary school," said Dad. "I think Mr. Benton wants to be with his boy and hear all about it, just like me."

As they walked up into the house, Steven turned to see T.J. and Mr. Benton bound up their steps and into their home.

Chapter 3

Dogs in the Grass

The first Saturday after school began was a hot, dry day. Grandma and Grandpa had been down for a week-long visit. They were leaving today.

The whole summer had been excellent. It was Steven's fifth summer in this house, the last house down a private road lined with tall oak trees. Most of the neighbor kids had been home all summer. The pool at the Grahams' house had been a popular spot. And almost every day they all played basketball at T.J.'s. He was getting really good, and so was their friend Travis, who bicycled over every day to practice.

Over the summer, Steven and T.J. had made lots of trips into the main areas of The Oaks neighborhood, seeking other kids to play with, Travis, Matthew Klein, the Sharp girls. But with the pool, and a shady area to play basketball, most of the neighborhood kids wanted to come here.

T.J. and his brother Chris had been home all summer except for a few days camping and surfing at the beach in Ventura. The Bentons were really into surfing these days, their side yard full of surf boards, wet suits hanging on the clothes line. It was dreamy and romantic.

Steven had a surf board. While he did not go as often as the Benton boys, he enjoyed surfing the mini breaks at Mondo's beach and carrying his board over to the Bentons' side yard for hours of waxing and surfer talk. Sometimes the older Cowan boys showed up. They were friends of Chris Benton and were excellent surfers.

Steven, T.J., and one of the Sharp girls had just started fifth-grade, the oldest kids in their school, Bedell Elementary. T.J.'s brother, Chris, their friend Travis, and neighbor Casey had started eighth-grade, their last year at middle school. Ally Sharp and the Cowan boys were in high school. It was all incredible. Where had the time gone?

Grandpa Russ and Grandma Janet came out of the house and joined Steven and his dog Petey on the front patio.

"Steven, we've got to go now. This was one of our favorite trips, ever," Grandpa said. "We enjoyed watching you kids play basketball, swim in the pool, surf, build things at the Scout-a-Rama, all of it. Most of all, I enjoyed trading fishing lures with you. But to get home before dark, your grandmother and I have to leave now. Remember, you're coming to our house for Thanksgiving. That's less than three months. Bring your favorite lures and we'll go fishing."

Steven hugged his grandpa and grandmother under the giant oak tree. Petey walked in a circle around the little group.

Petey bounded down the concrete steps into the gravel where Grandpa's white truck was parked. He went to the back of the truck and wagged his tail, in case Grandpa opened it and said, "Let's go, Petey." But that wasn't going to happen today.

"I love you Grandpa and Grandma," said Steven as they climbed into the front cab. Dad had said goodbye earlier. Now Mom came out of the house to give them one last hug and kiss.

As they drove away, T.J. waved goodbye from under his basketball hoop, his dogs, Kelsey and Maggie wiggling beside him. Steven was happy to see the old dogs out front, trying to have fun with T.J.

Steven ran over to the dogs and hugged each one. "Kelsey, Maggie, good dog," he said to each one. His younger dog, Petey, galloped over and peed in Mrs. Benton's flower garden, then went on a snooping and sniffing trip in their side yard.

Suddenly, the door flung open at the house between T.J.'s and Steven's and out came Casey, Melody and Jake with their dog, Millie, a spectacular female golden retriever.

"We're going to the field behind the Jones' house to get bugs for Jake's school project," yelled Casey. Casey's mom worked in Ventura and had their kids in school there.

"Can we come?" yelled T.J., assuming the answer would be yes. Steven and T.J. took off running into the brushy area between the Grahams' house and the Jones'. The dogs had stayed behind in the gravel driveway, sniffing each other and milling around. They were used to these kids running back and forth.

"Millie, come on," yelled Casey as she jumped from the low rock wall into the open field. This caused all the dogs to charge into the bushes after their kids.

Mom watched all this from the tall window next to her computer desk inside the house. "I'm so happy we live here," she thought. After checking her computer screen for a quick second, she looked back to the open field but the dogs and kids had vanished.

"How did five kids and four dogs disappear so quickly?" Then, far out in the field, the kids started popping up in the tall grass of the old farm yard.

"Okay," said Mom out loud.

"But, where are the dogs?" She could not see any of them. They must still be in the side yard, she thought.

All of a sudden, Mom saw the white tip of an all-black tail darting in and out of the green shrubs in front of the rock wall. "That's Petey," she thought. Over to the right, she saw a golden brown tail. "That's Millie."

Then, a skinny cream-colored tail and a tan one popped up from the weeds. "There's Kelsey and Maggie."

"Okay, all the dogs are still in our side yard," thought Mom.

Quickly, like a herd of deer, the dogs jumped the three-foot wall to join their kids in the farm field. First, black Petey, then golden Millie and finally creamy white Kelsey and tan Maggie. The three female dogs jumped onto the wall, then eased down to the farm field. Petey bounded over in one leap and charged after the kids.

Then a surprise, a huge white dog jumped up onto the wall. It was Bud, the Jones boys Great Pyrenees dog, thirteen years old. He must have been sleeping on their porch and heard the commotion.

"Hey, Bud! Come on!" Steven and T.J. yelled from far away as old Bud hobbled over the wall and trotted out to them.

"Five kids, five big dogs, amazing." Mom laughed. And with that, even Mom was a little sad that summer was coming to an end.

Chapter 4

September 11, 2001

Two weeks of school had gone by. The routine was set. Dad was out of the house before sun up to get on the road before the traffic was terrible. Mom was up by six o'clock and gave herself a half hour of personal time before waking Steven. Usually, she turned on the Today Show or Good Morning, America for five minutes of news.

On the morning of Tuesday, September 11, for some reason, Mom did not turn on the TV. That day, Dad had invited her to join him for lunch at a hotel on the beach where he was having meetings with people from Washington D.C. who were visiting the Naval Air Base where Dad worked. Mom was looking forward to the lunch.

After getting dressed, she fed Petey, let him out to pee, and played with him a little.

Mom didn't have to wake up Steven. He was old enough now to get up without help. He was ten years old, competent, and Mom was proud of him.

They each had a bowl of Cheerios and a fried egg. While Steven put Petey in the backyard, Mom went to her bedroom to put on shoes. They needed to leave the house in less than ten minutes, but Mom turned on the TV to see the headlines.

An airplane had crashed into the tallest building in New York City. The TV screen showed smoke and a lot of scared people covered in dust. As she watched, another airplane came onto the screen and crashed into the other tall building next to the first one. The TV announcers were saying things that were hard to understand because Mom had just turned on the TV. But the announcers were scared now. The fear in their voices was unmistakable.

Mom knew, she just knew, this was not an accident. This had been done on purpose by terrorists, people who wanted to hurt Americans.

Mom punched Dad's number on her cell phone. "Hello," she heard him say.

"Chris, have you seen what happened in New York City?"

"Yes. We are tracking every plane in the sky from our monitors. The computers we were going to use for our meeting can let us see every airplane over the

United States. We are helping to guide some of them to the nearest airports. We're doing some important monitoring right now. I have to go. But I'm told that our lunch will still be delivered at noon, so please come for that. I want to see you and so do the people from Washington you have met before."

"I love you. I'll be there."

Steven would be in school in a half hour and the teachers and other kids would know about this. Mom wanted to speak to him about it before anyone else. She had to explain the very scary things that had just happened and keep Steven from being afraid.

Mom turned off the TV and opened her bedroom door.

"Steven, come her for a second, honey."

Steven appeared. "What, Mom?"

"I had the TV on for a minute. An airplane crashed into the tallest building in New York City. At first, I thought it was an accident. Then a second airplane came and crashed into the building next to it. I think terrorists hijacked, you know, stole, the airplanes and flew them into those buildings to kill people and scare Americans."

It hurt Mom to realize that at age ten, Steven already knew what a "terrorist" was. She did not know that word until she was age seventeen, starting her senior year of high school. Terrorists took athletes hostage and killed them at the Olympic Games being held in Germany. In those days, if terrorists took airplanes, they usually landed them and let the passengers go. This was different.

"I'm going to turn on the TV and show it to you because your teachers, and maybe some kids, might talk about it at school and I want you to know what they're talking about."

Steven sat next to Mom on the bed and was quiet. She turned the TV back on. Smoke and dust filled the screen, more than before. Both of the tall buildings had disappeared into the smoke. Steven heard the worried voices of the TV announcers. Mom thought they sounded even more scared than before.

"Steven, we have to leave now to go to school and work. I'm sorry we have to go. Look, when you get to school, please don't talk about this, even if other kids are talking about it, all right? If someone asks you, just say you know about it and you saw a few things on television, okay? Because at school, some kid or even a teacher could have an aunt or uncle or a grandparent right now in New York City. We don't want to say anything that could make them more worried or more scared. Okay, honey?"

"Okay, Mom. I know what you mean."

Mom hugged Steven lightly. "This is terrible. But it happened far away from here and you don't need to be afraid."

"Okay, Mom," he sighed, and they went out to start their day.

Chapter 5

The Santa Paula Times

A few weeks passed. One evening Steven came in from playing basketball at T.J.'s. "Everybody had to go home because we all have homework," he said.

"You guys are doing homework on a Friday night?" Mom looked up from the salad she was making in the kitchen. It was early October and the days were shorter, but there was still light outside and the weather was warm for playing outside. Dad wasn't even home yet.

"We all have projects," said Steven. "Projects take a lot more time than normal homework."

"Fifth grade seems to have a lot more homework than fourth grade."

"That's for damn sure," replied Steven.

"Stop cussing! I mean it," Mom shot back. Mom walked over to the table and unrolled the town newspaper sitting at her spot.

"What's in the paper?" asked Steven nicely.

"Did you notice Petey brought in the newspaper about an hour ago?"

"I did notice," replied Mom. "It's wet in a few spots from his slobber, but it's not torn up like last time. Good job, Petey."

Petey got up off the floor and went to Mom. He knew the words "good job, Petey" meant he would get rubbed and hugged. Mom put her face next to his and gave him a squeeze.

Early on Wednesday mornings, a car came down the private lane and tossed a free Santa Paula Times newspaper to every house. That paper was full of advertisements for the local stores. But on Fridays, only subscribers got a paper. Mom was surprised some people didn't buy the Friday paper. It had the "letters to the editor." They were the talk of the town.

"Lots of good stuff in the paper," said Mom. "The opinion page is very mild today."

Since the terrorism of September 11 in New York and Washington D.C., people treated each other nicer, even in the Santa Paula Times newspaper. Everyone seemed more polite. The lead writer, a lady named Peggy, had always been a fair reporter. Mom thought that Peggy found ways to question politicians and authorities without accusing them. "That's a good skill," Mom said to herself.

At age ten, Steven kept up on local sports and even town politics. "Any nasty letters in there?" he asked his Mom.

"No, nothing you would want me to read to you," replied Mom.

"Any good sports pictures?"

Mom turned to the back pages and said, "Yeah, there are some nice photos from Junior Cardinals. No names, but I'm sure you would recognize every player."

Steven cruised over to the table before Mom could turn back to the opinion section. "Oh, that's a great picture of Stephen Klein rushing for a touchdown. I'll have to call Matt and tell him his little brother is a star in today's paper."

Yes, thought Mom, and she smiled.

Back on the opinion page, a few letters were a bit sharp, but no one accused anyone of bad deeds or outright stupidity.

"Hell, it's better to write a public letter than fight it out in the street," she said out loud.

"What?" came a retort from Steven at the computer desk where he worked on his science project.

"Nothing," said Mom.

The front page had troubling news. Reporter Peggy wrote of burglars stealing from people's homes, cars stolen, even a murder in one of the parks across town. How could this be, in our little gem of a town?

The criminal world did not exist here at the end of the private drive with our nice neighbors. This area seemed fine, all the way to school.

"At least no one messes with kids," she thought. "Kids are safe here, and dogs, too." And that made Santa Paula a gem of a town.

Yes, it was still a gem of a town. "Come here, Petey, and get some love."

Chapter 6

Bud Steals the Trash

The Grahams front door had a funny latch. It wouldn't lock or even close correctly, so Mom and Steven gently pushed it and hoped for the best when they went outside. Dad used a side door that had a proper latch. He didn't want the front door blowing open. Papers could go flying. Bugs could get in.

On a warm Saturday, Mom and Steven cleaned the pool. They had gone out the funny front door. Dad had gone to Boy Scout leader training and locked the good door behind him.

Petey ran to the backyard grass and flipped upside down to scratch his itchy body. Mom made piles of oak leaves on the pool tarp. She thought she caught sight of something white or whitish outside the wire fence on the Jones' side of their property.

Later, Mom said, "I didn't think it was anything, at the time."

Steven helped Mom move the heavy tarp that warmed the pool water.

"Pretty soon the water will be so cold you kids won't want to swim."

"I bet we swim all the way to Thanksgiving," replied Steven. "The ocean water is a lot colder than this."

"I appreciate your help," Mom said as she finished sweeping the dried oak leaves off the tarp and scooping them into the trash can. "I better get some swimming in. It's almost too cold for me now."

Steven saw that his mother was done and started towards the wooden gate to open it for her and their big can of leaves. Petey stayed behind in the yard beside the pool. He didn't want to be taken inside just yet. There may be squirrels to chase, you never knew.

"Mom, look at that!" yelled Steven as he opened the gate.

Mom had come up behind Steven and they both stared in awe as the Jones family's enormous white dog, Bud, who was thirteen years old, ran out of the Grahams' house. He had their plastic kitchen garbage bag in his mouth. Egg shells and paper towels went flying across the yard as Bud scampered towards his porch next door.

"The door must have blown open while we were back here and Bud went in the house! No wonder he's been coming onto our patio and looking at us through the low window," said Steven. "Look at Bud. I've never seen him run. I didn't know he could run."

"How can you get mad at a dog that does something like that?" asked Mom, as she started to laugh. "He's been up on our porch watching me at the computer a few times. I thought he was just lonesome when the Jones's were away. He knows we cook eggs on Saturday. He can smell them. That's why he attacked today. This is one of the funniest things I've ever seen."

"How did he get the plastic bag off the can?" asked Steven.

"Dogs are experts with their teeth," said Mom. "We better get a sack and pick up the mess. There are egg shells and paper towels everywhere."

After helping Mom, Steven ran over to the Jones's porch where Bud was licking his paws.

"Bad dog, Bud," he whispered. Then he laughed and hugged the big old fluffy dog.

Chapter 7

Miracles of Nature

Steven, Dad and Petey climbed out of the truck. They had been at Mill Park for the weekly Cub Scout and Boy Scout meeting. Scouts was just getting started after summer break. Dad was in his light brown uniform. Steven had just graduated from the blue uniform of a Cub Scout to light brown khakis like Dad's. Petey had on his uniform, a red Camp Three Falls bandanna.

Mom walked out to greet them on the chilly, dark October evening. Petey bounded up the concrete steps and into the house to check his dinner bowl. Mom closed the door behind Petey and started towards the gravel driveway.

"Aghhh!" Mom yelled. "I got spider webs all over my face!"

Every autumn, spiders appeared in the oaks. They filled the trees and spun their webs low enough to get into Mom and Dad's hair and faces.

Mom stopped and furiously brushed her face and hair with both hands. She brushed her neck and the front and back of her shirt.

"It's so dark now I can't tell if a spider got on me," she said. "Oh, what a bummer."

Mom never used the word 'bummer,' thought Steven. Her tone, and the use of that word raised Steven's natural defensiveness, even though his mother's attacker was only a bug.

"Did you get one on you, Mom? Do you want me to brush you off?" he called to his mom.

"Thank you, honey. I don't think so. I think it's just a lot of cob webs. They are so creepy."

Dad said, "They are the worst I've seen since we moved into this house. I don't remember the spider webs being as dense in past years."

Steven's fifth-grade class had a lot of science study and he found his parents' conversation about the spiders interesting. Plus, Boy Scouts involved a lot of science, and Chris Benton had mentioned the increased spider activity this year. Chris was a science whiz, thought Steven. He could teach fifth-grade science.

"Why would there be a lot more spider webs this year?" asked Steven.

Dad, who studied biology in college, said "Colonies of insects and even fish can have years where they explode in population. It could involve perfect conditions, after years of not enough rain, or something like warm temperatures after years of unusually cold weather. All kinds of reasons."

Interesting reasons, thought Steven.

Mom, who studied history and religion in college, said, "You remember how Moses in the old testament got the Israelites out of slavery in Egypt by bringing down hordes of flies and locusts as a punishment? And Moses turned the Nile River red like blood so the Egyptians could not have clean water to drink. Those could have been natural events, things ancient people couldn't explain and assumed God was doing to them."

Dad said, "The red water could have been plankton. Maybe the water temperature changed and a growth of plankton made the Nile River suddenly go red."

Steven remembered plankton from a trip to Mexico. They had gone out in a boat and white foam covered the water near shore. Mom wouldn't let Steven snorkel because she thought the foam was sewage from a broken pipe. Mom took no chances, being so far from home. Later, when they saw the foam far out to sea, Mom relented and let Steven swim.

"So, even spiders can have one year out of ten or twenty where they make a crazy amount of spider webs?" asked Steven, more to Dad than to Mom, not wishing to engage in Bible scholarship just now.

Dad said, "Yes, and it seems weird to us because, if you are only ten years old, you are seeing it for the first time. At age ten it seems unusual, but it really isn't. If you are twenty years old, you may have a distant memory of something, but it still seems abnormal."

Steven said, "Have you seen other things in nature that were big like that?"

"Yes, when I was a student on the island of Jamaica, I saw an ocean full of tiny sting rays, or creatures that looked like sting rays. There were millions of them in the water one morning. The day before there had been none. They turned the water black, there were so many of them," said Dad.

"How long did the water stay black?" Steven asked Dad.

"It's hard to remember, but it was more than one day. Probably two days, and then they all left."

"Where did they go?"

"They dispersed in the giant sea. When I saw them, they may have just hatched out of their eggs in the water, millions, maybe billions of them. The hatch lasted only a day or two, then they all swam away. But for a moment, it turned the blue waters of the Caribbean to black," said Dad. "It was a miracle of nature, just like these spiders in our oak trees."

"I'd like to see a billion baby fish turn the ocean black," said Steven.

"Just keep fishing and camping and eventually you will see great things," said Dad as they walked into the house.

Dad and Steven wrestled Petey to the rug and tried to get his doll baby toy from him. Petey was too quick and too sly to let them win. Steven hugged his dog with joy.

A few days later, Steven realized Trick or Treat was coming soon. He had always felt nervous going outside after dark when the spider webs hung low in the oaks. But after Dad described it as a miracle of nature, Steven said to himself, "I won't be afraid."

Mom had been right about the kids abandoning the swimming pool before Thanksgiving. It was only Halloween, but the cool nights had plunged the water temperature to below seventy degrees. Nobody wanted to come over and swim in the cold water. And the days were getting really short, so no one wanted to walk home wet, in the dark, under spiders webs.

So the pool was ignored except once a week when Mom asked Steven to help her get the dried oak tree leaves, dead spiders, squirrel poop, and just plain dirt off the tarp. Mom left part of the tarp off, to check the water. If it turned green, she would have to use algae-killing chemicals.

This morning was not a clean-up day, but Steven saw Mom at her bedroom window staring at the pool area.

"What's out there?"

"Come see at the window. Walk up slowly, next to me."

As a scout, Steven was well trained in stealth movement.

He stepped slowly toward Mom. Then he saw them. Three wood ducks were swimming in their pool! The morning sunshine exploded their colors of green, cinnamon and golden yellow. Two were males and had green crested heads with long neck feathers that looked like little helmets. Their faces were striped in black and white. They were the most beautiful ducks in North America.

"Mom, I read that wood ducks look for standing water under trees, and they like to eat acorns. Maybe these ducks were migrating south for the winter and saw the huge amount of acorns we have in our trees right now, and our pool down below."

"I didn't know they hunted for acorns," said Mom. "And I definitely didn't think wood ducks might fly over our swimming pool and think it was a lake. These three ducks have been coming for a couple of days, but not every day. I wasn't sure I wanted to tell you, and disappoint you if they didn't come back. But here they are."

"It's great to see them close up," said Steven. "Their colors and markings arc amazing in the sunshine. I wonder if they came from Mr. Wilson's pond over on Cliff Drive. It's big enough for migrating ducks to hang around for a while. Maybe something scared them off for a bit and they came here to hide out."

"That could be."

Steven said, "Look at them. We have another miracle of nature."

Chapter 8

Acorns Cover Us Up

Petey roared into the living room. What was that noise outside? Steven was sitting at the computer next to the glass windows watching acorn nuts suddenly fall from the oak trees. It looked like black hail, and sounded like a million golf balls hitting the roof.

"Wow," yelled Steven.

"I know!" laughed Mom as she walked out from the kitchen into the living room. "That is amazing."

"It's covering the whole patio, Mom. Look, the white concrete is totally covered with acorns!"

The acorns had been falling for about a week. As Halloween decorations appeared in people's yards, the acorn nuts began to explode out of the oak trees in their famous neighborhood known as "The Oaks" of Santa Paula. And this was an amazing year for acorns. All the neighbors' yards were covered. Their patios up to the front doors were covered in acorn nuts.

Dozens of squirrels came scampering into the yard to pick up the acorns and chew, chew, chew. The squirrels Steven and T.J. had watched as babies jumping through the trees last spring were now full grown and racing through the branches, harvesting as many acorns as they could. Winter was coming and the squirrels needed to eat and fill their bodies with nutrition to get through the coming cold weather.

"I was planning to use the leaf blower to get rid of the acorns tomorrow when you're in school," said Mom. "But I think I'll do it today. There are just so many of them."

"Can I save some of them?" said Steven.

"Why do you want them?" said Mom.

"I don't know," said Steven. "They're just so interesting. There are so many of them."

Mom said, "I know. I have never seen anything like it. We have been in this house over five years. Every year there have been acorns in the autumn. But this year, they are crazy. There are buckets of them. Remember all the spiders we've had and Dad talking about the millions of sting rays he once saw in the ocean? Maybe this is the year of the acorn, not just the spider. One more miracle of nature."

Petey and Steven stood at the window looking out at the hail of acorns. The noise they made hitting the roof scared Petey and he let out a howl.

"Don't be scared, Petey, said Steven, "It's just a bunch of nuts coming from the sky." And he reached down to hug Petey and make him feel safe.

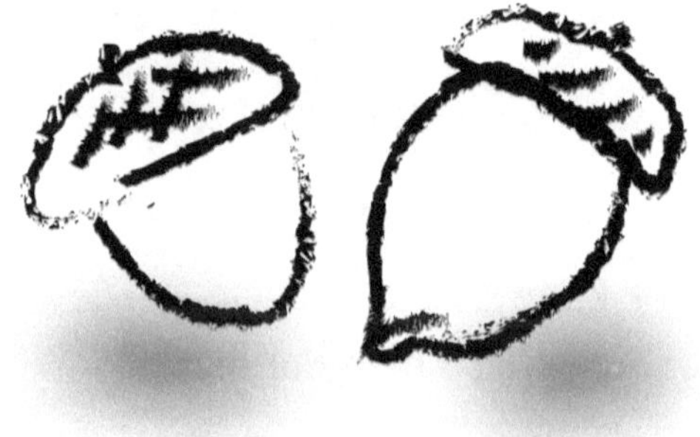

Chapter 9

Baseball and the Holidays

The World Series of baseball pitted the defending New York Yankees against the Arizona Diamond Backs. The awful terrorism of September 11 set the games back a week, the first time World Series games would be played in November, just a few weeks before Thanksgiving.

The series opened in Arizona and the D-backs took a fast two game lead thanks to a dominating pitching staff. The Yankees won game three.

Arizona was far away from New York and Washington D.C., where the terrorists had smashed buildings and killed Americans. Watching the World Series from a stadium in Arizona let everyone relax a bit, and just watch baseball.

But when the series moved to New York, the country worried that other terrorists were still out there, scheming to hurt the United States again. Would they come to Yankee stadium and hurt a baseball crowd? The whole country wondered.

"Look, Mom, the stadium is full!" said Steven, in front of the TV.

Both Mom and Dad said, at the same time, "That is great!"

Mom said happily, "Look at all the American flags. It's red, white and blue all over the stadium." Mom was at the kitchen table packing a few pots and pans she would need to help Grandma cook Thanksgiving dinner in just a couple weeks.

The President of the United States walked onto the grass for the ceremonial first pitch. The state of New York had not voted for him to be President, but these New Yorkers cheered loudly. It meant a lot to have a President come to their damaged city. He waved to the crowd and strode to the pitcher's mound, the first President ever to throw from the distance.

The President threw a perfect strike into the catcher's mitt. The Yankees crowd erupted in cheers.

Dad said, "He was once the general manager of a pro team, the Texas Rangers, so it doesn't surprise me this President can throw a strike, even from the mound. Not like those Presidents they have to move up ten feet so they don't throw the ball in the dirt."

Steven and Mom laughed at Dad's remark and

watched the patriotic pregame show. The perfect strike had taken the worry away.

Soon, Roger Clemens replaced the President on the mound. Two hours later, Mariano Rivera closed it in the ninth for the Yankees, and series was tied.

Petey looked at the TV and then at his family. He always knew when the show was over.

"Come get a rub, Petey," said Dad from his chair. Petey got a round of rubs and hugs. His people had been extra loving to him since September 11, but he felt their tension. Petey was on alert, he just didn't know why.

Every day the TV showed pictures of smoking ruins in New York City. People were still missing and presumed to be dead under the rubble of the World Trade Center buildings. Families taped pictures of their missing loved ones on fences around the area. It was a very sad time. Mom kept the TV off except for sports and a few movies.

The Diamond Backs beat the Yankees in game seven, in a dramatic bases-loaded walk-off single by Luis Gonzales.

Deep into November, the Grahams packed the mini-van and headed to Thanksgiving dinner at Grandma and Grandpa's house in Northern California.

The freeway was jammed with cars.

"I think people are afraid to fly in airplanes. They're all on the highway," said Dad as he eased onto Interstate 5 from the lovely farm fields of State Route 126.

Petey knew where his "pee stops" were on this route. He'd been to the grandparents' house many times. They drove through the hills known as the Grapevine and onto the southern tip of the great central valley of California. Dad turned into the gas station just below the hills.

"Settle down, Petey, settle down," said Dad as the happy black dog jumped up and down in the back seat. It was pee stop number one.

Mom turned around and hooked Petey's red leash to his matching red collar, getting him ready to storm out of the van.

"Let's go!" yelled Mom. Out they poured into the vacant lot next to the gas station. Dad headed to the pump and then to the men's room. Steven saw that Mom had taken charge of Petey, so he sneaked into the market for candy and chips.

Mom caught up with Petey and unleashed him to run free. The sleek black dog ran like a racehorse. At the edge of the lot, Petey found a patch of weeds and lifted his leg to pee.

"Go poop," yelled Mom. She knew Petey would feel better on the rest of the trip if he was "empty."

Petey was still a young dog. He ran and ran, stopping just to pee a few times.

That's all he did. No number two.

"Oh, well," said Mom. "Let's go, Petey," and the dog raced to the car and leaped in next to Steven.

Soon, Dad turned onto State Route 99 through the central valley farm towns instead of Interstate 5.

At the town of Pixley, Dad stopped near some duck ponds. Petey lumbered out of the car and ran to the weeds by the road.

"Yay, Petey did number two," said Steven.

"I'll pick it up," said Mom, who always carried a plastic grocery bag during a Petey stop.

"Not necessary," yelled Steven. "I put a big rock on it."

Hours later, they pulled into Steven's grandparents' driveway. The sun was shining on the back of the house. The front was shady. Neighbors' trees were bright red, yellow and cinnamon against the blue sky. Thanksgiving was the most beautiful time of the year in Northern California.

Petey ran to the door, wagging his tail and wiggling his whole body, greeted by Grandpa at the screen. He'd been here many times before. The two of them disappeared into the living room for wrestling, hugs, and new toys.

The kitchen was filled with aromas of fried potatoes, onions and pork chops. Little bowls of salad were on the dining table.

"Wash your hands, wash your hands," shouted Grandma, happily. She knew her travelers would be hungry and they'd head straight to the table. Everyone thought this meal would be almost as wonderful as Thanksgiving dinner tomorrow.

Over the next several days there were long conversations about the Yankees losing to the Diamond Backs. Steven and Grandpa evaluated the pitchers. It was all about the pitching.

Petey played at the park behind Grandpa's house. The blue and white kingfisher appeared. The Grahams saw the bird scouting for crawfish along the little creek that ran through on the far side. The dark green grass was lush and damp. The Grahams sneaked Petey off his leash when no other visitors were there. He jumped from rock to rock across the little creek.

Mom gave Petey his special whistle signal when she saw people entering the park. Petey ran to her and she fastened his leash. He got a rub and extra praise for being good.

"Petey, you are the best dog!" whispered Mom. Petey wagged his tail furiously. He wiggled his whole body.

That Saturday, Grandpa drove Steven, Mom and Dad to Grizzly Island wildlife area to look for elk, pheasant and bald eagles. Petey stayed home with Grandma. He could not run around in the wildlife area. His chances of getting turkey scraps from Grandma were good.

A month later, Grandma and Grandpa made the trip south to Santa Paula for Christmas. It was colder and wetter in December, even in Southern California. Grandpa's truck carried a ping pong table in a box, topped with a big red bow, Steven's Christmas gift. There were many other gifts and bags full of treats.

"Petey! You came out in the dark to welcome us," exclaimed Grandpa as he got out of the truck. "And look at your pretty red and green Christmas collar!"

It was only four-thirty in the afternoon, but

the days were short. Deep shade made it seem like nighttime under the oak trees. All the neighbors' Christmas lights were on. The Grahams had Frosty the Snowman on their roof surrounded by lights.

"I'm glad you were able to drive down for the holidays," said Mom to Grandma when they were all in house.

"I agree," Grandma said. "I still wouldn't want to fly on an airplane right now."

Later that evening, Grandpa got out an old photo and sat down on the sofa.

"Steven, I found this old picture of Berlin, Germany, taken when I was there in 1948 and 1949. I was 20 and 21 years old at the time. That's me in the picture. I spent Christmas of 1948 there.

Everyone got up to look at the young Grandpa. A buddy of his had taken his picture on a street that had many destroyed buildings.

"Was that during the Berlin Airlift?" asked Steven. Mom had told him the story of the starving German people after World War II. The Russians were on our side in the fighting, but problems came up later and they blocked the roads into Berlin. No food or supplies could get into the city. The Americans did not want the German people to starve after they had stopped fighting.

"Tell us again, Grandpa, what did you carry in the planes?" said Steven.

"We might have a plane load of potatoes," said Grandpa. "On the next flight it might be coal to heat people's homes."

"Grandpa, did you drop little parachutes with Hershey bars out of the airplane windows?" Steven loved this story and want to hear it again. He knew American airmen made toy parachutes from handkerchiefs. They tied pieces of kite string and old shoe strings onto the ends of the cloth. Then they tied on the candy bars. When the American planes flew over Berlin, the pilots dropped the toy parachutes carrying candy to the children below.

Grandpa said, "I did not release them from the plane. But I made the parachutes and tied the candy bars onto the strings. When the pilot said he could see kids down below, your grandpa handed him the little parachutes to toss out the window."

"Oh, Grandpa, I just love that story," said Steven. Now I can't wait for Christmas.

On Christmas morning, Grandma and Grandpa

watched Steven and his friends play basketball at T.J.'s hoop. It was foggy white outside and looked like a Christmas card. The basketball players seemed to glide like ice skaters on a pond. A black dog with a red and green collar danced around them. The perfect turquoise sky of Southern California was replaced with white fog on Christmas day.

That night, Steven rolled an old baseball to Petey and said, "Well, Petey, wasn't Christmas nice? It will be baseball season before you know it."

Chapter 10

Dad Gets New Grass

On a cool late January day, Petey and Dad went to the backyard together. Things looked terrible. The grass seed Dad had spread last summer never turned into lush grass. What they saw now was a mix of weeds, grass and dirt.

Petey didn't mind the bald spots. He had created some of them. The soft dirt was cooler than the grass in summer time and less scratchy.

Last week Mom had said, "We planted seed to get beautiful grass and to keep the dog clean, but now Petey comes into the house covered in dirt."

"Come on, Petey, let's go downtown." With that, they marched down the steps to the gravel driveway. Petey sat beside Dad and they headed to Frank's Paint and Hardware.

But first, Dad stopped at Santa Paula Coffee Company for a large, take-out coffee. Petey jumped into the driver's seat to watch Dad. It only took a couple of minutes and the weather was chilly, so Dad knew did not worry about Petey waiting in the truck.

Dad returned and nuzzled Petey. "Okay, let's go," he said as they backed out onto Main Street. Three blocks up on the right was Frank's. The Manzano family had bought the paint and hardware store when Frank retired, but they kept the name. The Manzanos were a big sports family in town.

Petey was welcome in the hardware store, so Dad hooked the red leash to the dog's matching collar.

Mrs. Manzano was in the store. "Good morning. Can I help you?" She recognized Dad, but couldn't remember his name.

"Do you still sell rolled up turf grass?" asked Dad.

"Yes, it's outside. We don't have much in the store, but we can get the amount you need in only one day."

"Great," said Dad. "I'll look at what you have," and he and Petey went into the garden area to look at the different types of grass.

Three types of sod were rolled up like rugs on a shelf. Dad saw what he wanted. Mrs. Manzano had followed him out and Dad told her the size of their yard.

"Mr. Graham, I can have all the sod you need when we open tomorrow. Do you have all the other things you need for the job?"

"I believe I have everything else," replied Dad. He paid a deposit for the order and thanked Mrs. Manzano.

Petey jumped into the truck and Dad closed the door. "You stay, I'll be back," he said, and walked briskly into Brilliante Market next to Frank's to get Petey a string cheese.

Dad noticed La Terraza Café at the end of the block.

Opening the truck door, Dad said, "Petey, let's get some Chili Colorado to take home."

La Terraza was on the best corner in town, Main Street and Tenth. Everyone drove through here, coming or going. The café had a large outdoor patio.

"Corn or flower tortillas?" said the high school girl who took Dad's order.

"Harina," said Dad, repeating one of the few words of Spanish he knew.

She smiled and continued in English, certain that Mr. Graham didn't speak much more Spanish. "Any soda or iced tea?"

"Yes, two diet sodas, thanks," said Dad as he paid and guided Petey over to a table along Main Street. The new translator program in his phone told him "refrescos" was the Spanish word for "soda."

Petey snooped around the patio to the end of his leash.

"Petey!" some child yelled from a passing car. Petey wiggled his body.

"Yay, Petey," came more yelling. Dad smiled.

"Petey, you're famous in this town," said Dad as he reeled Petey back to him for a hug and kiss.

"Here's your order, sir," said the young employee, walking out to the patio table.

"And refrescos, too?" asked Dad.

She gave Dad a big smile, held up the drinks and said, "Refrescos, too, sir!"

Chapter 11

Minor A Sign-Ups

On a cold Saturday morning in February Petey nuzzled Steven at the side of his bed. It was like "Get up, get up, we have things to do today." How did Petey know?

Steven could smell hot grease wafting in from the kitchen. Must be pancakes, he thought.

Lately, Steven was having a hard time getting up early on Saturday mornings. It was hard to get up for school, too. On school nights, he had to be in his room ready for bed at eight thirty, but often he didn't fall asleep until much later.

Even on nights when he fell to sleep quickly, the mornings were brutal and his body wanted to melt back into the soft mattress.

From the kitchen, Steven heard, "The snack bar opens at eight o'clock for sign-ups. You and Vince going down early? I don't have to be down there until later."

This reminder sprung Steven to life. He dove for his flip phone and punched Vince Montoya's house number. Vince did not have a personal cell phone, yet.

Mom had told him, "You only have a cell phone because it's like a pager. If I call you on that phone, you must answer or call me back immediately, or you can't keep it." Steven kept to those rules because having a cell phone was great.

Vince politely answered his house phone. This was in the days before phones announced who was calling, so Vince didn't know who it was.

"It's Steven. You want to go down in twenty minutes to Harding Park to sign up for the A's?"

Both boys knew they'd get picked for Coach Garcia's A's. Steven, Petey and Vince had been on Garcia teams since their first year in baseball. But they still had to sign up and Richard Ruiz stadium was the place to be today. All the players and coaches would be mingling and talking baseball, a great day of camaraderie, showing off, and good wishes all around.

"Okay, twenty minutes. My dad said he'll drive us," said Vince.

"Great, see you in twenty."

"Mom, can I have three pancakes, some bacon

and a glass of milk?"

"You certainly may," came the deep voice of Dad from the kitchen. Petey had already left Steven and was milling around close to the stove. Dad had fed the dog earlier and decided the people of the house needed pancakes this morning. Petey was hoping to get a piece of bacon or, worst case, a dog biscuit from the box.

Steven dropped to his knees beside the refrigerator and hugged Petey. The dog spun around in a circle and then jumped up and down.

Steven looked around for Mom. She was making her bed.

He called to her, "Dad put the butter out so it's probably very soft and he put our milk in the freezer. It should be just the way you like it in a couple of minutes."

Every family had it's weird food rituals, thought Steven. It was a favorite thing of his to check out other family's customs when he ate with friends. Serving soft butter and ice-cold milk were two of his family's strange food habits.

Steven had already pulled on last year's uniform and ball cap. Everyone would be in last year's gear until the new uniforms arrived in about a month.

Dad delivered a short stack of hotcakes to his plate on the table and Steven dug in.

"You have some, too, Dad," said Steven. Without realizing it, Steven began more Graham rituals of dining, such as inviting everyone to sit and eat together. Steven's eyes scanned the table looking for something Dad or Mom might need when they sat down. Did they have forks, butter knives, coffee? Yes, all those things were there.

Dad said, "I'll be right there with a stack for your mom and me."

Mom came in from the bedroom and sat down. Petey flopped down on the carpet near the table, one eye open for any action that might involve a snack. Petey knew this was an excellent time to be good. Good dogs got nibbles.

Just then, Martha Brown's little dog, Jackson, streaked by the side window on his way to freedom, that is, until Martha caught up with him. Everyone looked the other direction and, sure enough, Martha arrived on the Grahams' steps in hot pursuit. She lived in the first house, on the corner of the Ojai Road and their private drive.

Through the window Martha saw them all at the breakfast table and stopped. All the Grahams waved their arms and pointed behind the house, the direction Jackson had run. Martha took off. Petey charged to the window, barking and jumping up and down. From time to time, Jackson escaped from his house. He loved Petey and always headed this way. The Grahams finished their breakfast, knowing Martha would scoop up Jackson quickly and carry him home in her arms.

Just then Mom notice forty pink flamingos in the front yard, plastic ones on sticks. "Look at that! Mrs. Benton flew her skate park birds into our yard."

T.J. and Chris's mom had organized a charity for the skate park. It was a huge hit all over town. Early in the morning, Mrs. Benton drove to someone's house and stuck forty pink flamingos in their yard. The cute birds stayed there for a week. That family was then asked to make a donation to "fly" the flamingos away to someone else's yard. The skate park was getting the funds it needed and the whole town was having a ball try to guess where the birds might "land" next.

"Petey and I saw them early this morning," said Dad. "I'm surprised you didn't notice them until Jackson and Martha came through."

"A lot going on around here," said Steven. Mom laughed. "Yes."

A few minutes later, Mr. Montoya's black truck came down the private lane and Steven was waiting. They all waived bye to the Grahams.

"I'll be down after a while, "Mom yelled as a reminder. Mom was on the board of Santa Paula Little League. She filled in at activities that needed extra help, like sign-ups. She liked to joke, "As long as I stay off the field they allow me to serve!"

Mom asked Dad, "Can Petey stay here with you for a few hours? Sign-ups will be too crazy for him, I think."

"Sure. Petey and I will inspect our property, stack some wood, and take a nap."

"He will love it," said Mom. "Bye. I'm off to the world of little league."

Mom eased the van out, turned onto Ojai Road and quickly stopped at the side of the road. She made a call, waited for traffic, then ran across to a small blue and white house.

Bob Flores was at the screen door. "Thanks for calling," he said. "I didn't have a ride until later, so I appreciate going with you, Rita."

"I've missed you over the winter, Bob," said

Mom, and she and Coach Flores sped off to little league sign-ups at Harding Park.

Mom dropped Bob at the umpires' private table near third base. She steered the van toward the snack bar in the back. The shack was belching smoke from fried egg sandwiches on the grill.

"Menudo is on the way," someone said. "We'll heat it up and put it in coffee cups for sale."

There was a line of ten or twelve kids and parents waiting to sign up for baseball. Mom grabbed a clipboard and registration form. She called up the next player, signed him up, and told his parents the date of try-outs.

A truck arrived. The line parted and everyone got out of the way when several big boys carried up two stock pots filled with menudo. A hush came over the snack bar helpers. Joy spread in the line outside.

That night, Mom placed a call to Mrs. Benton. "Melanie, when it's time to fly the flamingos, I want to send them to Bob Flores' house around the corner. And I want to pay for his "fly away." Bob has been a retiree for a long time, so I don't want him to get stuck with the fly away fee."

"Happy to do that," said T.J.'s mom. "Nobody has to pay the fee. It's just a donation for those that want to donate. But I appreciate you doing that."

"I want Bob to get them and not worry about what to do. It will be great to see the pink flamingos on Ojai Road. Bob has one of the best locations in town for this."

"He sure does," said Melanie. "I'll sneak them over early next Monday morning in time for rush hour. They'll be there all week. It will be great."

That Monday, Mom drove Steven to school, but turned left instead of right at the end of the private lane.

"Where are we going?" Steven asked.

Before Mom could answer, the van passed the Flores house. Bob's tiny yard was covered with pink flamingos and he was out in his bath robe and house slippers looking them over, with a big smile on his face.

"It looks like a hundred of them!" said Steven.

"It really does," said Mom. "Let's keep it a secret who sent them to Bob's yard, okay?"

"Totally," said Steven. "T.J.'s mom is magnificent. She is a master organizer of good things."

"Totally," said Mom.

Chapter 12

Try-outs

A month later, the stadium came to life on try-out day. All the players crowded the stands at Richard Ruiz field to watch Minor A tryouts. Steven and Vince Montoya were already "picked" on the Garcia family team, the A's.

Coach Ralph would be back as manager. His nephew, Aaron was trying out today. Aaron's dad, Chris, would be their new on-field coach. He was young and athletic. Steven liked him. Aaron's mom, Claudia was one of the great young moms of Santa Paula Little League.

Ralphy Junior was twelve and already in the Majors. Big Ralph was staying down in the Minors with the A's.

Steven and Vince thought they might have to officially tryout, so they wore their beat up A's uniforms from last year with the hard-earned stains. Mr. Montoya had given them a lift over to the field.

Aaron was called to the infield by the announcer. He handled all six hits from Cardinal manager, Rey Fernandez, who always ran tryouts. Aaron expertly snagged each ball and fired to first. His fielding performance was impressive. The crowd of players, especially A's fans, hooted their approval loudly.

Aaron hadn't developed as a pitcher, but from the mound he managed to throw four strikes out of five pitches. The sixth pitch snapped into the catcher's glove, a fastball strike, and all the A's players behind the chain link fence shouted to Aaron, "You're the man, Aaron!" They applauded him to home plate for his batting tryout.

Steven said to Vince, "Watch him bat. I think he's the best nine year old hitter in town." Aaron went to the dugout for his bat. Coach Rey strolled to the mound and threw six pitches, all strikes, down the middle.

Aaron connected on all of them. The fifth pitch he drove into center field, smacking the wall for a near home run. The green-clad A's players stormed the fence and clung to it with fingers and hands, shouting approval to Aaron.

"Will the spectators please return to their seats," said the voice of the announcer.

Every Minor A team had to pick at least three nine year-olds. Steven shouted, "We want that nine year old!" Everyone laughed because they knew Aaron was a Garcia and the A's were the family team.

Coach Chris hugged his son at the dugout and told him he had done a great job. They returned to the stands and rounds of high fives.

After a few more players, the announcer called up "Alan Quinn." Out came a chunky little Mexican kid dragging a bat. A thin man with red sunburned skin wearing a T shirt and jeans stood at the first base fence.

"Where's Quinn?" somebody yelled.

"That is Quinn," yelled back a different voice. Nothing more was said because everyone in Santa Paula was used to the mix of Mexican and Anglo families.

Steven said to Vince, "Alan is the smallest player trying out."

Vince yelled out, "Hey, Quinn, T-ball tryouts were last week. You're late!" The kids roared with laughter.

Alan trotted out between third base and short. Coach Rey scorched a grounder, much harder than he intended. Alan snapped it up and fired to first base, crack, into the glove. Alan had everyone's attention.

Five more hard grounders, and he fielded all of them expertly.

"What an arm," said Steven as the crowd applauded this boy. The twelve year-olds helping Coach Rey gave Alan thumbs up.

Alan walked up to the mound for his pitching try-out. Coach Rey tossed him the ball. While his speed was a moderate change-up velocity, all six pitches were strikes. Not one player had thrown six strikes. The crowd applauded.

"Way to go, Alan," they yelled.

Coach Rey called Alan to the plate, gave him his bat, and took his glove. "I'm going to throw you six pitches, all strikes. Do your best to hit the ball. Good luck."

Alan nodded as Coach walked to the mound.

Alan punched four hard grounders in a row past the infield. More applause from the stands. Coach Rey's fifth pitch was in the dirt. Little Alan thought he was supposed to swing at every pitch, so he did, and fell down hard.

"Woops!" somebody yelled from the bleacher side.

The remorseless gaggle of ten year-olds screamed with laughter. Parents gave them the "hush-up" look. Coach Rey ran in from the mound to check Alan. Mr.

Quinn just stood confidently by the dugout fence.

Alan got up and said to Coach Rey, "I'm good."

The next pitch was an easy slow ball over the plate. Alan cracked the ball to center field. A player shagging balls had to jump for it.

"That's a double in a real game," said Vince. "I'm impressed."

Steven said, "I guess that's why they let him try out for Minor A's. He can hit. Fields and throws pretty good, too."

Before the boys finished their evaluation, the sixth pitch came down. A loud crack shot through the stadium. Kids rose from their seats.

"It's over! It's out of there!" they yelled. The big kids roared and the gallery of ten year-olds sat with their mouths hung open. This was a massive, out of the stadium home run. Twenty kids ran to the Boys and Girls Club to find the ball and parade it back.

Coach Rey's staff of twelve year-olds poured in from the outfield and the dugouts to congratulate the little hitter.

"Dude, want to try out for the Majors?" joked Steve Trejo, a star on the White Sox.

All the parents shouted and clapped, Mrs. Quinn and Alan's sister with them.

Behind the chain link next to the first base dugout, Mr. Quinn hugged little Alan and said, "Nice job! Good tryout."

In the stands, Steven and Vince agreed. "That was epic! Where is Coach Ralph? Somebody tell him to draft Alan Quinn!"

Chapter 13

Big Pollen

About the time baseball got started, the trees and grass in the Grahams' yard got going, as well. Dad came in from mowing the grass. He had grass all over him and yellow pollen in his hair. Oak tree pollen made Dad's nose run. He went straight to the box of tissues and blew his nose, very loudly. Petey came in from Steven's room where he was sleeping, but the big noise worried him and he did not go over to Dad.

Suddenly, Dad realized he was dropping pollen from his shirt all over the floors. He backed outside, took his T shirt off and shook it five or six times. Petey followed him outside. Dad dusted off his jeans and stamped his feet. Petey got a little excited, thinking something fun was about to happen.

"Come here, dancing dog," Dad said as he put his shirt back on. Petey jumped up and put his front paws on Dad's chest. Dad allowed Petey to jump on him. Petey understood Mom did not want to be jumped on, ever, and it was okay to jump on Steven as long as he didn't knock him down.

"What are you doing, what are you doing?" Dad said over and over to Petey and rubbed his face. Petey jumped down and ran around Dad in a circle.

Steven and T.J. came running up the concrete steps when they saw the commotion. Like Petey, they thought something fun was about to happen.

"What are you going to do now, Dad?" said Steven, knowing Dad was finished mowing the grass.

"Nothing. This pollen is bothering me. My nose won't stop running and my eyes are watering. Do I look like I'm crying?"

"Yeah," said T.J. "You do!"

Every spring, pollen suddenly appeared all over the oak trees around their houses and down the private drive. At first, it looked like pretty yellow flowers. When the flowers fell off, the tree leaves had thousands of fuzzy stems. This was the pollen.

The pollen dropped out of the trees and covered the patio. On a windy day, the pollen would make piles four or five inches deep around the trees. It got all over their cars. Mom and Dad had to turn the windshield wipers on, not for rain, but to brush away the yellow pollen.

Mom got the leaf blower out every day and blew pollen away from the doors and windows so it wouldn't get into the house.

"I wouldn't like this if it lasted more than three or four weeks," she told Steven. "But I know it will end soon, and the trees will be even prettier."

"Yeah," T.J. said to Dad, "I hate the pollen. It gets all over me. Look at my red eyes. But I'm used to it."

Steven said, "Look, even Petey's eyes are a little bit red."

"Yeah, the pollen monster is going to get us all!" yelled Dad as he chased Steven and T.J. back down the steps. "Help me drag these garbage cans to the carport and I'll drive you guys over to Ray's Market for a strawberry jarrito."

"Yeah!" they yelled and ran to the trash cans. Petey circled Dad's truck because he knew more fun was about to happen.

Chapter 14

Return of the Racoons

Grandma and Grandpa drove down the Grahams' private lane late in the day. Easter was early this year and the temperatures were still cool. It was the Thursday before Easter. Even though the days were getting longer, the sun was already over the hill, and a long shadow was over the house and yards.

Grandpa's truck tires made a crunching noise as the big white vehicle pulled into the spot next to their sailboat.

Mom opened the front door of the house for Petey to run out and greet Grandma and Grandpa.

Steven was in the backyard, but heard the truck arrive and the sound of Petey storming into the gravel driveway.

Steven abandoned the camp he was making in the back and ran to his grandparents.

Mom watched from her computer desk next to the big glass window. She smiled as Steven greeted his grandparents and Petey also made them feel welcome and loved. Mom let them have time with each other before walking down to hug her dad and mother.

Steven was saying, "Grandpa, you need to see my racoon hunting camp in the backyard. The racoons are back."

Grandpa said, "I want you to show it to me. But first let's get all of our bags out of the truck and into the house. Will you help me?"

"Of course," said Steven. "Just fill my arms with your bags."

"I'll help too," said Mom, as she walked down the front steps and took a sack from Grandma.

As they walked toward the house, Steven said to his grandfather, "We have racoons, Grandpa. They come in the night and they're tearing up the grass again in the backyard."

"Yeah?" said Grandpa.

"Yeah. It's a long story," said Steven. "Remember, Dad got turf grass for that dead spot in the back yard. He prepared the dirt and laid down the rolls of turf. We watered it. It was beautiful. And then, in the morning of the very next day, we went out there and something had rolled up the grass and torn it apart. You should have heard Dad," said Steven.

"I bet," said Grandpa. Grandma had gone into the kitchen to talk with Mom.

Steven continued, "You know Mr. Benton is a farming expert. He told Dad it was probably racoons. He said there are grub bugs in the soil and the racoons know it. They roll up the grass and claw it apart to get the grubs, to eat them. The racoons keep returning. Dad said he is going to get some chicken wire and lay it down over the grass to keep the critters out, but he won't have it for a few days. The racoons have been coming every night. So T.J. and I are going to camp out on the patio and shoot them with our BB guns. Petey is camping, too. Do you want to camp out with me, Grandpa?"

"Not tonight, I'm too tired from driving."

"Okay," said Steven, "But come and see my camp." They walked out to the fenced area around the swimming pool. Steven had set up his personal Scout tent and the Grahams large family tent. His sleeping bag was spread out in the small tent. The larger one held the Daisy BB gun, a box of BBs, walkie-talkies, a small cooler with two bottles of water and a big bag of M&Ms, and one of Petey's old beds.

Grandpa said, "Have you seen the racoons?"

"No, but Mom has. She told me the pool lights woke her up last night and when she got out of bed to turn them off there were six racoons around our pool. A couple of them reached into the water to wash their paws. Can you believe that? But the craziest thing was, Mom said the racoons saw her and some of them came over to the window. She said they weren't afraid and two of them stood up on their back legs to look at her. Mom said they waved their little arms. I guess it was really their front legs they waved. She said it looked like a slow motion dance. Isn't that weird?"

"Yeah."

"Sure enough, this morning, the racoons had dug up the grass again, the grass that Dad has been trying to keep nice. So he's fed up."

"Are you going to shoot the racoons with the BB gun?" asked Grandpa.

"Yep. T.J. is coming over with his BB rifle and we're going to camp out and keep those racoons out of here."

After dinner, Steven ran over to T.J.'s house and the two of them returned carrying T.J.'s supplies. Grandpa and Grandma dashed out into the chilly night to see if the boys needed anything, but didn't stay long. Dad walked out with a lantern for the boys. Petey pranced around Dad trying to figure out if he was supposed to stay with the boys or help Dad. Petey decided to help Dad and go back into the warm house.

Steven and T.J. chose to camp together in the Grahams' tent. It would be warmer.

From inside the house, the grown-ups got up to check the tent from time to time. The lantern stayed on for about an hour. The boys turned it off about eleven o'clock. By then, everyone was asleep, except for Mom. She turned on the pool light so the boys wouldn't be afraid if they woke up in the middle of the night. Mom didn't sleep well that night, but when she got up to look outside, the racoons weren't there; just the little tent camp in the dark corner of the back patio.

Before the morning light came into the bedroom, Mom heard a small commotion outside the window. T.J. was dragging his sleeping bag towards the gate and Steven was out in the grass with Dad.

She heard Steven say, "They came when we were sleeping! And they tore everything up again! I can't believe it."

"Yeah, I came out as soon as I woke up," said

Dad, "You guys were fast asleep in your tent. I saw that the racoons had come in the night and done their dirty deed once again."

At breakfast nobody made fun of Steven. They were all surprised the racoons were so tricky. They had all slept through it.

Dad knew Grandma and Grandpa were still tired from the long drive so he slipped out quietly to the Santa Paula Hardware. Luckily the store was open early and had chicken wire in stock.

By early afternoon, Dad, Steven and Grandpa had laid out the wire over some new turf and secured it around the edges with bricks from a pile they kept out by the stone wall.

"That ought to keep those dirty racoons out of here," said Dad.

"Yeah," said Steven.

"Yeah," echoed Grandpa.

But down deep in the ground, under the chicken wire, a new little critter, known as a mole, had just discovered the soft, luscious dirt under Dad's new sod.   He couldn't wait to show off his tunnel-making skills to the people above. He'd start tonight, now that the racoons were gone for good.

Chapter 15

Petey and the Baby Squirrels

Petey bumped the glass window and banged against the door. It was rather unusual. He was a calm dog now that he was older, especially inside the house. Unless he was in the middle of a play fight with Steven or Dad, this banging around was not normal.

Mom heard the dog's commotion and came out of the kitchen. "Petey, what are you doing?" Petey jumped, ran in a circle, and whined loudly.

Mom walked over to the big window. Suddenly, she understood why Petey was jumpy. A dozen baby squirrels were in the oak trees chasing each other. Yesterday they hadn't been there. This morning, they had taken over the trees, chasing each other, jumping from branch to branch, squeaking and screaming.

Mom open the door and Petey burst out, stopping under the huge tree next to the concrete step. Somehow, Petey thought he could get these squirrels, but he quickly figured out they were way above him. He couldn't reach them. So he leaned his front paws high on the tree trunk and barked like a crazy dog.

Mom didn't like Petey howling outside, but this was a dog's prerogative. How dare these squirrels show off in Petey's yard!

Petey ran to the other big oak in front of the house and yelled at the squirrels the way a dog yells - bark, bark, bark.

Steven ran out of his bedroom where he had been sorting baseball cards. It was early on Saturday morning and he hadn't presented himself to the household yet. But Petey's unusual barking brought him racing into the living room.

Still in his pajamas, Steven ran outside and saw the riot of squirrels. "Where did they come from?" he yelled.

Steven was used to squirrels in the trees, but this was wild.

"I think they're the babies of the big squirrels that were here over the winter," said Mom. "It's springtime and I think they were born in those big nests high up in the trees."

Steven had noticed the big nests, but he hadn't known they were full of baby squirrels.

"This is great! I'm going to call T.J."   And Steven ran back into the house to the phone on the desk.

"T.J., this is Steven. We have a thousand baby squirrels in our trees. Come over."

T.J. said, "I got five thousand of 'em in our trees behind the house. They woke me up at five o'clock this morning. Can't you hear my mom's new dog, Foxy, barking like crazy?"

Steven looked out his window and saw little Foxy bouncing up and down in the Bentons' large front window, the one that displayed the most beautiful Christmas tree in the world during the month of December. Now it was March, and the little head and neck of Foxy was going boing, boing, boing up and down in that window.

"Yeah, I can see that dog right now in your front window. I guess it heard Petey going nuts. Come over. Does Chris want to come over and see these squirrels?"

"My brother is still sleeping. An hour ago he opened one eye and said he has seen the hatching of baby squirrels in our trees a bunch of times and he wasn't getting out of bed for them today." Chris was in junior high and needed more sleep than a couple of fifth-graders.

"I'll talk my Dad into taking us to McDonald's

for breakfast. Come over," said Steven and hung up. He knew that would get T.J. over here.

"I heard that," said Dad as he walked out of the bedroom in his pajamas, heading to the kitchen to make coffee.

"Can we, can we, can we?" Steven said sweetly.

"I'll consider it after a cup of coffee," said Dad as he disappeared into the kitchen. "Somebody go out and get Petey before the neighbors call the police," joked Dad. At least Steven thought he was joking.

"Mom's out there with Petey. She's got his red leash and is chasing him, but he's having too much fun."

"That doesn't sound like fun," said Dad. "Sounds like Petey wants to massacre any squirrel that gets down low enough on a branch where that dog can get it, or a squirrel that falls out of a tree jumping from branch to branch."

Steven planted his bare hands on the window glass to see if that was happening in his yard. If that was happening, he didn't want to miss it.

Instead, Mom had corralled Petey and was leading him from the grass to the concrete patio and the front door. Steven could see T.J. slamming his front door and bolting across the basketball court to the Grahams' house.

"When Petey saw Dad through the window, he knew he better get in the house," said Mom. "He thinks he doesn't have to obey me but he always wants to please Dad."

T.J. followed Mom in and said "My Dad said I could go with you to McDonald's!"

"Well, then, I guess we better," said Dad. "Let me get my pants on and we'll go! Those squirrels aren't going anywhere."

Chapter 16

Petey Likes Cheetos

Petey got up from his dog bed after an afternoon nap. It had been hot and there was no air conditioning in the house. Petey stretched his front legs out in front of him and lowered his chest almost to the ground. His back legs stood tall.

It was late in the afternoon and Steven was home from school. School would be out for summer in a month.

"Petey, you look like Mom doing yoga," said Steven as he walked over to hug his awakening dog. Petey let Steven grab him and roll him over onto the ground to play. Steven scratched and rubbed Petey's belly and Petey lightly kicked with all four of his legs. With his front legs, Petey boxed Steven more vigorously as Steven lightly slapped the pads of his feet. Petey knew he could play fight Steven more furiously than with Mom or Dad. Petey knew Steven liked it.

Mom walked out of the kitchen with a little bowl of Cheetos. Petey sprang upright and galloped over to her.

Steven said, "Petey, where you going? Oh, you want a Cheeto!"

Mom flipped a Cheeto into Petey's mouth, then another one. Petey wagged his tail and then wiggled the whole back end of his body.

"Do you think Petey knows the word 'Cheeto'? said Steven.

"I haven't worked with him to learn 'Cheeto,' said Mom. Petey did not know very many words. He mostly watched the members of his family and tried to figure out what they wanted him to do.

"Can I have a few Cheetos to take out on the patio to teach Petey?" asked Steven.

"Sure," said Mom as she returned to the kitchen to supervise how many Cheetos Petey and Steven were going to get. Mom knew Steven would be eating most of them.

"Lay out five or six of them on the patio table so you don't accidentally eat a Cheeto that's been in the dog's mouth, okay?"

"I'm not dumb, mother," said Steven.

"Sometimes you are. We all are," replied Mom. "When we try to do too many things at once, for instance."

Steven took the bowl. He and Petey ran out onto the patio.

"Cheetos," said Steven as he dangled one above his head. Petey was smart. He did not jump or go crazy. He sat.

"Good boy," said Steven and lowered his hand to put the Cheeto in Petey's mouth.

Now Petey ran around Steven, prancing and jumping.

"Sit." Petey sat.

Steven gave him a second Cheeto. And another one and another one. Soon all of Petey's Cheetos were gone.

"Good dog," said Steven as he held up the bowl to his mouth and let his tongue scoop up the rest of the cheesy treats.

Chapter 17

Steven's Home Run Ball

The A's rolled that season. Hot pitchers. Clutch hitters. Steven was a decent pitcher, a dependable hitter, and one of the best catchers in Minor A.

But he hadn't hit a home run yet. Almost every other serious player his age had hit one. Mom wondered if he was aware. Oh, he was acutely aware.

Petey continued going to every game. He had a fan club of little kids and big sisters of the players. Kids would lay out special blankets for Petey to sit on. He wore a pink tiara and got his nails polished. They fed him pieces of their hot dogs.

"Petey, you're the king!" laughed Mom. Two or three other parents heard that and laughed, too.

It was the last regular season game, the A's versus Astros. A's were ahead eight to one in the top of the fifth inning. Steven was catcher for the game and now up for his final at bat. Lalo was umpiring and signaled "batter up."

After two outside balls, Steven took the third pitch, a medium fastball down the pike.

Crack! Mom, Dad, Petey, and the A's fans all looked up. The outfielders were positioned deep. It looked like the left fielder would raise his arms and get this. But the ball carried, and softly dropped over the fence.

The crowd wasn't sure. Mom wasn't sure. The only one sure was all-star Steve Trejo, of the Major Division White Sox, sitting in the stands with his teammates, waiting for their game later than afternoon.

Before the ball dropped over, "Steve T" bolted out of his seat and began a full on sprint towards the Boys and Girls Club. He knew what a home run swing looked like and what a home run crack of the bat sounded like.

Umpire Lalo lifted his arm, pointed his finger to the sky and began the twirl that announced "home run!"

Steve T was joined by a dozen other players, fans, Petey, and some dogs from the parking lot. Off they stormed to the back of the stadium to get the home run ball.

It was a solo homer. Steven rounded the bases to his parents' standing ovation. Other A's parents clapped and cheered. Now the score was nine to one.

Mom said to Dad, "I can buy him a home run trophy! That's great. That's just great!"

"Yeah, it really is," said Dad. "Steven deserves it. I better go get Petey. Where is his leash?"

"It's on him," said Mom. He took off at a hundred miles per hour with twenty kids, leash flying, tiara flying."

"Mmm," said Dad as he eased down the concrete steps to the chain link fence.

Mom happily accepted high-fives from other A's mothers and waited for the half-inning to finish and the Astros to come up for their last outs. She saw Dad had fetched Petey and she saw him standing outside the fence at the third base dugout with the dog next to him. All the kids from the home run stampede had stayed out there to watch the finish.

What happened next was little league crazy, the reason everybody came to the games and stayed. The Astros came up and scored three easy runs. They scored on a wild pitch, two errors, and a few great hits.

Within minutes, the score went from nine to one to nine to eight.

With two outs and two on, the Astros batter smacked one hard to the short stop. He decided the best play was the runner who had taken off for home.

Steven stepped in front of the plate, waited for the ball and, like a dozen times before, put a blistering tag on the runner.

Lalo signaled "out." But the runner plowed hard towards the plate, knocked Steven's left arm and the ball came loose.

Steven went over hard onto his back. He rolled up quickly but a second runner had rounded third and was heading to home plate.

"Safe," corrected Umpire Lalo, with his arms out to his side, high-stepping out of the way of the wreck at home plate. Tie game.

"Where is the ball?" Steven thought. It was behind him. He saw it and dove down as the second runner stormed in. Steven scooped the ball with his catcher's mitt and bare right hand and spun his arms into the runner who was now upon him.

"Safe. Safe!" yelled Lalo, wildly swinging his arms straight out. Game over.

"Can you believe that?" thought Mom silently. The A's fans sat stunned and quiet. Dad, Petey and the crowd moved up towards the concrete bleachers.

Petey and Dad made it to the stands and sat next to Mom. Below, Mom saw White Sox star Steve

Trejo politely moving past the fans to get to the other side, the A's dugout. He moved like a professional athlete, quick and tall.

Steve T disappeared around the back of the dugout where the A's were leaving. Mom saw the boy walk out with her Steven. He patted Steven on the shoulders, smiled, and headed away towards his White Sox buddies.

Petey pulled Dad towards Steven. They walked to the dugout with most of the A's parents. Mom stayed behind. From far away, she saw Steven bend down and hug Petey. She knew her boy was fine.

The beauty of baseball, she thought, was the number of games in a season. Most of the time players got to experience both winning and losing.

Steven ran up to his mother in the stands and said, "Look, Mom, Steve Trejo found my home run ball and gave it to me. The best baseball player in our league made sure I got it."

Hours later, Steven was fast asleep in his bed. Petey snored on the floor next to him. Mom looked at the home run ball on the desk and thought about the excellent boy who'd made sure they got it.

She said, "He's a Santa Paula boy. A gem of a kid from a gem of a town."

Chapter 18

The Brawl on Laurel Road

Dad was home from work on a Friday. He had just finished mowing the grass. It was late May and the grass was growing fast in the long sunny days. Dad would have to mow every day for the yard to look perfect. But he mowed once a week, and the yard still looked pretty good.

Only that dastardly mole could mess things up. Secretly, Dad thought the mole was very interesting. He didn't do as much damage to the lawn as the racoons. He just left one line of raised dirt and grass as he ran around underground. So Dad just watched him and gave reports to the family from time to time. Steven would be home soon and he'd show him the mole's latest movements under the earth.

Down on Laurel Road, school had just let out and kids were pouring out of the school yard. Steven, Matt Klein, Quinn Palmer and Zach McMillin formed a squad meandering down the road, but moving quickly.

Up ahead Steven saw Diego Canto with a buddy.

Steven lost sight of them when they turned right on Los Robles Drive. That street cut directly through to Ojai Road. Diego lived across the road.

Quinn pushed Zach and Zach retaliated with a running jump directly at Quinn. It sent them both tumbling into the lush grass of a somebody's yard.

"You guys could have gotten impaled on the fence," yelled Matt at his wild buddies.

Zach was punching Quinn, but they were both laughing.

Steven thought Quinn could knock Zach out with one punch if he wanted to. Quinn was getting to be a big kid. But Zach was fast. He rolled away on the grass and sprang to his feet like a dog. Steven laughed at that move.

Other kids walked around the madness to get home.

Cecilia Marlowe and her girl pals from third-grade paraded down the middle of the street, believing, as they should, that none of these boys would accidentally bump into them.

"Cee Cee!" You better watch out! These guys are off the rails. They'll knock you girls down." Steven was very protective of his good friend Travis's little sister.

The girls kept chatting loudly. Steven thought he heard a bit of laughter from them, but they kept moving straight down the street to her turnoff on Woodland Avenue. It amazed Steven that the girls weren't scared of mayhem in the street. Ever since the Sharp girls moved to Texas, Cecilia and her little crew had taken over. They were girls to be protected and admired by boys who knew their dads and moms. "Our girls," thought Steven.

Steven saw Cee Cee's little dog, Dexter, poke his face out onto Laurel Drive from Woodland Avenue. He let out a little "woof," and the girls took off running to him.

"Well, good," thought Steven. They're out of the . . . whap!

Out of nowhere, a grapefruit smacked Steven up the side of his head. Steven staggered over to the grassy yard where Quinn and Zach stretched out resting now that their "fight" was over.

"Day-um!" yelled Quinn. Zach jumped to his feet.

"What got me?" yelled Steven. His eyes stung from grapefruit juice. He could barely see and was a little scared. Steven laid down on the grass next to Quinn. "Am I bleeding?"

No other kids were around. Steven's pals looked left and right two or three times. Suddenly, Matt Klein yelled, "It's Diego!" He turned around on Los Robles and threw that grapefruit off a fruit tree!"

"No kidding!" yelled Zach. Matt and Zach took off running towards Diego. Diego took some fast steps down Laurel then spun around and ran up through some yards towards Quinn and Steven. Matt and Zach couldn't get him because he darted behind some bushes.

Steven felt a rush of adrenaline. He popped up and charged towards the oncoming Diego.

Quinn yelled, "Hey, Diego, that was awesome. You threw a strike on Steven's face from fifty yards. You want to be on my majors team next fall? We need some pitchers." Quinn rolled over on the grass and laughed.

Diego had no time to respond. As he ran out from behind a tree, Steven flew at him and knocked him to the ground.

Quinn howled, "Hey Steven don't hurt Diego. I need him on the White Sox. Besides, he didn't mean it. No fifth-grader can throw a strike from a hundred feet with a grapefruit. He got lucky."

By this time, Mr. Marlowe had poked his head around from Woodland Drive to see what the ruckus was on Laurel Road. His daughter Cecilia was safely out of sight.

Zach saw Mr. Marlowe and decided to perform a flying kung fu kick in the direction of Diego's head, without making contact, of course. Mr. Marlowe let out a grunt, turned around and left. Laurel Road, down by Woodland, that's where all the shenanigans happened.

Meantime, Steven had dragged Diego down to the grass and landed a hard punch to his head.

Steven thought, "I may have hurt him," but his schoolmate didn't react or even flinch. Having spent years in First Baptist preschool, Steven was a reluctant fighter, but public school was wringing that out of him.

The boys tumbled and each landed some punches to the face and chest. And then they stopped.

Diego was huffing and puffing but he wasn't hurt. He had a tiny fleck of blood around his lower lip. Steven had the start of a black eye.

Quinn, Zach and Matt were on the grass in the next yard. A few other boys had walked up and sat in the yard waiting for Diego or Steven to start crying or get knocked out. They would carry the kid home to his family as needed.

"Alright, Steven, I'll see you at school tomorrow," said Diego. "I got homework to do." And he got up and trotted off.

Steven looked at him. Besides the split lip, he'd put a good grass burn on Diego's knee. Diego limped a little as he ran toward Los Robles and his way home.

"How do I look?" Steven asked his pals. He couldn't show up at his house all bloody. "Is my shirt torn?" There would be too many questions from his parents, and he wasn't in the mood for that. The left side of his rib cage hurt, but not too bad. He could feel dirt on his face and something wet, either blood, tears or snot.

Matt took off his T shirt and wiped Steven's face. "You're good. No cuts. Maybe a black eye coming."

Zach sprang over to where Steven was sprawled on the grass, grabbed both his arms and pulled him up.

"Let's get out of here. You guys live in such a bad neighborhood," laughed Zach as he ran towards Ojai Road.

"Yeah, I'm not up for basketball over at Bentons," said Matt as he turned back up Laurel. I'm going home."

Quinn put his arm around Steven and said, "I'll walk you home. Middle School is out today and I came over to your school to talk to some future White Sox players. Baseball's over but we're going to practice this summer. We need to beat the Cardinals again next year."

Quinn waved to Steven as he turned down the private drive. Steven could see Dad in the one-car garage putting away the lawn mower.

"Hi, Dad, I'm home."

"Hi, Bud. Your face is a little dirty. Did you fall down?"

"Yeah," said Steven as Petey ran up and nuzzled his legs.

Chapter 19

Petey Goes to Middle School

Petey was still an escape artist. And he had gotten better at it. After four years living with the Grahams, he knew when they got home, no earlier than a quarter till three.

Petey typically left the yard at eight and joined some nice ladies on their morning walk through the Oaks neighborhood. Sometimes he extended his guided excursions down to the houses behind the school. He once escorted a lady to a beautiful home way up on Ojai Road.

Later, he would walk home, jump the fence into his backyard and be asleep in the shade when his family came home. Oh, the praise he would get for being a good dog and staying happily in the backyard all day.

Once in a while, one of the ladies was so helpful, Petey would get invited to her home. She'd put him in her backyard. A call was made to the Grahams' house, using the phone number on his collar. Mom would drive over and get him around three, after hearing the recording on the machine saying where he was. He would get a lecture during the car ride home, "Petey, no. Stay in your yard."

Other times, Petey would hang out in some nice lady's yard, take a swim, play with her dogs, and after a while jump their fence and walk home. Mom was often confused to find her dog at home while the message machine said "You can come get your dog."

Dad was threatening to get Petey a dog sweater that said, "I'm on my way home; I don't need to be rescued."

One day, Petey showed up on the playground of Isbell Middle School, a mile and a half from the Grahams' house, past downtown.

Petey was resting in the shade of a tree. Bobbie Benavides was the first kid to spot Petey.

"Hey Chris, isn't that Steven Graham's dog?" said Bobbie to Chris Benton who was nearby. Bobbie and his little brother Anthony played baseball. Bobbie knew his brother played with this dog at the Little League park and loved him. He also knew the Bentons and the Grahams lived across the private lane from each other.

Chris walked over. "Yeah, that's Petey." At the

sound of his name and the smell of his neighbor boy, Petey jumped up and put his front paws on Chris's chest.

"Petey, what are you doing here? Is your mom here?" Both Chris and Bobbie looked towards the school parking lot for Mrs. Graham's brown minivan. It wasn't there.

"Petey, you better go back home. They'll call the dog catcher on you," said Chris, who knew all about Petey's unauthorized travels around town.

"I'm surprised to see him all the way down here," Chris said to Bobbie. "I don't want to tell the principal. They'll call Ed, the dog catcher and Petey will have to ride around all day in his hot truck. He might even get taken to the Camarillo dog shelter. It's happened before."

Bobbie said, "I'm going to hide him. My little brother loves this dog and I'm not going to let anything happen to him."

Just then, the assistant principal saw the dog in the school yard and half-ran to the boys.

"Get away from that dog," he ordered.

Chris said, "That's my neighbor's dog. He must have gotten lonely and followed me to school. He's a friendly dog."

The administrator said, "Get away from the dog. I know nothing about that dog. A dog cannot be in the school yard with all these kids. It's the rule."

Petey was happy to have another friend and ran in circles around this new person. The administrator turned and walked towards the office.

Chris said to Bobbie, "Let's put him out the gate. He'll walk home. I am one hundred percent sure of it." Chris steered Petey to the school yard side gate and out to the sidewalk. But he didn't leave. Petey wanted to come back in the yard and play.

Chris said, "Bobbie, I'm going to my class. If we just leave, that dog will go home. Don't worry about him. Trust me. He does stuff like this all the time." Chris walked back to the classrooms.

Bobbie looked at Petey outside the chain link fence. Petey wagged his tail vigorously. That was it. Bobbie opened the gate and grabbed Petey. Then he took off his belt and made a leash and fastened it to Petcy's red collar.

The school bell rang for the next period and Bobbie had five minutes to figure out what to do.

Bobbie yelled to a kid on the playground, "Go find a bowl and get some water for this dog."

The boy saw the dog and took off. Boys will always help a good dog. In one minute, the kid was back, running with a plastic bowl, water sloshing out.

Bobbie said, "Excellent." He had walked Petey to the shade of a huge tree a little closer in. Bobbie set down the water bowl.

"Petey, I have to go. You stay. And I'll be back in forty minutes. Stay put."

He walked away, but turned around and said, "Stay." Petey stayed.

Bobbie was in his math class. Chris was in science two classrooms away. Suddenly, Petey was at the open door of Bobbie's classroom.

The teacher was very nice, "Did somebody lose a dog? Is someone's parent here and this dog got away from them?"

Bobbie's mouth fell open. "That's Steven Graham's dog, and Mrs. Graham's dog." He assumed everyone in town knew them.

"Is Mrs. Graham here right now?" asked the teacher.

"Yes," fibbed Bobbie. "She may have gone home because Petey got away from her, but Mrs. Graham knows he's here."

"Hmm," said the teacher.

Bobbie started to sweat. He did not like lying to a teacher, but something caused him to become Petey's protector right now, at all costs.

"Chris Benton knows he's here. Chris lives right across the street from Petey's house. He's an eighth-grader. Can he just get out of class a little early and walk Petey home?" Bobbie was ready to battle the system to save Petey from the dog catcher.

The teacher left the room and returned with Chris, who smiled when he saw Bobbie. "Did he follow you in here?"

"Yes," Bobbie said. "I asked my teacher if you could take Petey home."

"That's not going to happen," said the teacher. "And the dog cannot stay."

Just then, the bell rang for the end of that period. All the kids in Bobbie's class surrounded Petey. He ran circles around them and bowed low to get hugs. The kids loved him.

"But everybody knows Petey and we know where he lives. We can't let the dog catcher take him away," Bobbie told her. Some other kid yelled, "No!"

The assistant principal came to the door. "I'll take the dog," he said.

Suddenly, Bobbie bolted from the classroom. He knew Petey would follow him. Petey stormed out after Bobbie in a full gallop back to the school playground.

"Go, Petey, go," yelled some kid.

The adults did not panic or yell, but Chris Benton threw his head back and laughed as he turned to go to his final class.

"Bobbie, you can't have this dog at school," said the assistant principal when he found the boy and the dog sitting under the tree.

Bobbie knew it was true. He got up, took off the leash, hugged Petey and walked slowly back to the classroom. He felt he had let down his little brother, Anthony, who loved this dog.

Petey wanted to stay in the shade and rest. As the assistant principal reached down to grab his collar, Petey jumped up and ran. He ran down the side of the fence looking for a way out. He ran between the buildings and out to the front plaza. Petey hid among the vehicles parked on the street.

The assistant principal was a nice man and did not call the dog catcher, but he decided to make an announcement on the school's public address system.

"Your attention, please. There is a large black dog loose just outside the school grounds. Do not approach the dog. Do not try to touch the dog. Come to the office if you see the dog."

In his classroom, Chris Benton said to himself, "You've got to be kidding me."

Then, he saw Petey in the school yard at the window of his classroom! Chris said to the teacher, "May I be excused to go to the restroom?"

"Of course," said his teacher.

Chris ran around the building and whistled to Petey. Petey was by his side in three seconds. Chris took off his cloth belt and made a leash like the one Bobbie had made. He slipped it around Petey's collar.

"Let's go, Petey." To where, he did not know.

Chris walked by an eight-grade classroom and saw Travis Marlowe. He did not see a teacher.

Chris went in and every head in the class looked up.

"I found this dog and am taking care of him," Chris announced to everyone.

"Petey!" someone yelled. All the kids knew him.

"Travis, where's your teacher?"

"She's gone for about five or ten minutes. But she'll be back."

"Well, in ten minutes school's going to be out for the day. I've got to get back to my class. Can I stash Petey here?"

"Of course."

Petey was tired and sprawled out on the floor next to Travis's desk. Everyone stayed in their seats and smiled. The ones closest to Petey reached down to pet him.

Honk, went the final bell, just as Travis's teacher came into the room. Then Bobbie rushed in and said, "I got word he was in here with you, Travis. I'll take him."

"You sure?" said Travis.

"Yes. We've protected him so far. I've decided to take him to the front of the school and find some Mom who will drive him home. Somebody will do it."

"Okay, I'll help you," said Travis. "Come on, Petey." The whole class charged out of the room with their dog.

"Be careful, students," said the teacher. "See you tomorrow."

Petey got loose from Bobbie and Travis. He roared through the crowd of Moms, students, and little brothers and sisters. No one screamed. No one was afraid of the friendly dog. A tiny girl said, "Petey."

Petey smelled Chris Benton somewhere in the crowd. As Chris climbed into his mother's silver van, Petey leaped in next to him. Mrs. Benton had already picked up T.J.

T.J. yelled, "Petey, how did you get here!"

"We've been hiding him at school all afternoon," said Chris. "He showed up in the school yard and the kids hid him so the principal couldn't call the dog catcher."

"Really?" said Mrs. Benton in the driver's seat.

"Really," said Chris. "Craziest thing I ever saw. And we're talking about Petey."

"Well, close the door, and we'll take him home," said their mom. Mrs. Benton had her own stories about the adventures of Petey. There was that Sunday afternoon when Petey jumped out of the Grahams' backyard and walked the entire circuit of the Annual Garden Tour alongside the ticketed patrons.

Petey sat upright in the van next to Chris, watching the traffic. He was looking for Mom's brown minivan and the boys knew it.

"Look, Mom, I got a limo ride home! Woof, woof!" snarked T.J.

His brother erupted in laughter. Mrs. Benton shook her head.

Petey rose up on all fours when they turned onto the private drive.

"Sit down Petey, you're beating my face with your tail," said Chris. T.J. laughed.

When Chris opened the door, Petey flew out and raced to his house across the street.

Steven had just pulled up from school on his skateboard. Petey almost knocked him over.

"What happened?" he yelled to his friends.

"You wouldn't believe it!" both Chris and T.J. yelled at the same time. And Steven stood there in the driveway with his great dog, his great friends, and all of them had their mouths hanging wide open.

Chapter 20

We're in Middle School Now

There were some science projects to finish. Baseball was still on. The days were getting longer, and kids played outside after dinner, waiting for the complete freedom of summer. On every street in the neighborhood kids were out in the cool air of late spring. Fifth grade was almost done.

T.J., Matt Klein, Vince, and Steven were sitting in the back of the Grahams' sailboat parked in the gravel lot. Petey was underfoot. The boys stretched their legs and sipped on bottles of lime Jarritos. They knew the adults around the private lane could see them, but not hear what they were saying, which was good.

"I'm not looking forward to Isbell next year," said Matt.

After a long pause, T.J. said, "My brother says it's okay." He wanted to comfort his friend.

"Yeah, well, he won't be there. He'll be at Santa Paula High School."

"Yeah, yeah," murmured T.J. He agreed it would

be good if his brother had another year at the middle school they were going to.

"It will be okay," said Vince. My sister went there. But I think it is rougher now than when she was a student.

They all gave Vince a look that said, "Thanks, Vince, that's very reassuring."

"My parents are sending me to St. Augustine down on Wells Road," said Steven. Almost all the students are Santa Paula kids. I'm kind of looking forward to it."

"I wouldn't mind going to St. Sebastian for sixth grade," said Matt, "but my parents think Isbell is better academically."

"Yeah, I wouldn't mind going to St. Sebastian," said T.J., and the boys all laughed because T.J. wasn't Catholic or a member of any other church.

"I don't think you have the prerequisites," joked Vince.

"Are you guys scared to go to Isbell?" asked Steven. "I heard some of the big eighth-graders beat up sixth-graders when they can get away with it. You think tha true?"

"Nah, nah, nah" said Vince. You have to be an

a-hole to get beat up. So, just don't be one."

"So, how do you feel about that, my friend, Matt?" asked Steven.

"I just don't know," said Matt as he let out a sigh and reached over to pet Petey.

"Yeah," his buddies agreed, all at the same time, leaning back in the boat. "I just don't know," each one said to himself.

The End